2

PRINCESS Kitty

The Royal Ball

by Melody Mews illustrated by Ellen Stubbings

LITTLE SIMON
New York London Toronto Sydney New Delhi

LITTLE SIMON

An imprint of Simon & Schuster Children's Publishing Division

1230 Avenue of the Americas, New York, New York 10020

First Little Simon hardcover edition February 2020. Copyright © 2020 by Simon & Schuster, Inc.

All rights reserved, including the right of reproduction in whole or in part in any form.

LITTLE SIMON is a registered trademark of Simon & Schuster, Inc., and associated colophon

is a trademark of Simon & Schuster, Inc. For information about special discounts for bulk

purchases, please contact Simon & Schuster Special Sales at 1-866-506-1949 or

business@simonandschuster.com.

The Simon & Schuster Speakers Bureau can bring authors to your live event. For more

information or to book an event contact the Simon & Schuster Speakers Bureau at

1-866-248-3049 or visit our website at www.simonspeakers.com.

Designed by Laura Roode. The text of this book was set in Banda.

Manufactured in the United States of America 1219 FFG 10 9 8 7 6 5 4 3 2 1

Library of Congress Cataloging-in-Publication Data

Names: Mews, Melody, author. | Stubbings, Ellen, illustrator.

Title: The royal ball / by Melody Mews ; illustrated by Ellen Stubbings. Description: First Little

Simon paperback edition. | New York : Little Simon, 2019. | Series: Itty Bitty Princess Kitty ;

#2 | Summary: Newly-crowned Itty Bitty Princess Kitty is delighted that there is to be a royal ball

in her honor, until she learns that she must perform, then teach, a dance. Identifiers:

LCCN 2019022088 (print) | LCCN 2019022408 (eBook) | ISBN 9781534454965 (pbk : alk. paper) |

ISBN 9781534454972 (hc : alk. paper) | ISBN 9781534454989 (eBook) Subjects: CYAC:

Cats—Fiction. | Animals—Infancy—Fiction. | Princesses—Fiction. | Balls (Parties)—Fiction. |

Dance—Fiction. | Fantasy. Classification: LCC PZ7.1.M4976 Roy 2019 (print) |

LCC PZ7.1.M4976 (eBook) | DDC [E]—dc23

LC record available at https://lccn.loc.gov/2019022088

LC eBook record available at https://lccn.loc.gov/2019022408

Contents

A Royal Wake-Up Call

Knock-knock.

"Are you awake, Itty?"

Itty Bitty Princess Kitty yawned. "Yes, Mom," she murmured sleepily.

"Don't fall back asleep in that cozy new bed of yours," the Queen called from outside her room.

Itty giggled. Her new bed was part of a whole new bedroom that was fit for a princess. Just

yesterday she had simply been Itty Bitty Kitty. But then her eighth shooting star had arrived, which meant that today—and forever—she was Itty Bitty Princess Kitty, Princess of Lollyland!

Itty got out of bed and walked toward her new closet. She paused in front of the display case that held her glowing shooting star.

Itty couldn't believe how beautiful it was.

And she still couldn't believe she was a princess. Some of the changes, like her new room, had excited Itty. But others, like getting a new hairdo or being palace-schooled, hadn't. Those changes had made Itty worry she wouldn't feel like herself anymore. Luckily her parents, the King and Queen of Lollyland, had explained that she

could be the princess she wanted
to be. She didn't have to change
her hair or be palace-schooled.

*I'm glad I still go to school
with my friends,* Itty thought.

And now that she was thinking of school—she didn't want to be late! Itty opened her huge new closet and chose an outfit. She was almost downstairs when she heard her mom calling her.

"Don't forget to make your bed!"

Itty ran back to her room. As usual, she'd forgotten to do her chores. A teeny part of her had hoped that maybe, as a princess, she wouldn't still have to make her bed . . . but it seemed chores weren't changing either!

The Almost
Announcement

In the schoolyard Itty's friends, Luna Unicorn, Esme Butterfly, and Chipper Bunny, rushed over to greet her.

"Tell us everything, Princess Itty!" Luna squealed, glitter flying everywhere. Luna's horn sprayed glitter when she was excited.

"Well—" Itty began.

Suddenly, Pansy Panda rushed over. "Your shooting star was so beautiful!"

"Thanks," Itty replied. "I—"

Harper and Fawn, deer sisters, nudged their way to the front of the crowd that had gathered.

"How does it feel to be a princess now?" Harper asked breathlessly.

"Um, well—"

Suddenly their teacher, Miss Sophia, rang the bell. Everyone knew what that meant. It was time to head inside for class.

"I'll talk to you at recess!" Itty told her classmates.

Itty, Luna, Esme, and Chipper headed to their classroom in the rainbow wing, while Pansy, Harper, and Fawn trotted off toward the spiral staircase that led to their classroom in the clouds.

Itty and her friends settled in to their seats. Because it was the beginning of the day, the desks were red. The desks in the rainbow wing changed color every hour

when the Lollyland mermaids sang. So the desks were red in the morning and violet when it was time to go home.

"All right, everyone," Miss Sophia said with a big grin as she stood in front of the class. "I know we are very excited about Princess Itty's shooting star, but it's almost time for second bell, so . . ."

Just then, Itty noticed an announcement fairy sitting on her desk. The tiny fairy was waving her little arms, trying to get Itty's attention. The last time an announcement fairy had shown up, she had announced that Itty was about to become a princess!

Realizing that Itty had finally seen her, the fairy raised her miniature trumpet . . . and at that moment, the bell began to ring.

Itty could see the fairy's lips moving but couldn't hear anything she was saying. The fairy finished her announcement just as the bell stopped ringing. Then she flew off before Itty could ask her to repeat what she'd said. Itty had not heard one word of it.

News from the King and Queen

Itty was still thinking about the announcement as her desk turned from orange to yellow. What important news had she missed?

But she barely had time for another thought about it, because the rest of her day was packed with lessons, questions from her classmates about being a princess, and excitement about an upcoming field trip to Cloud Park.

By the time the desks turned violet, Itty had *totally* forgotten about the missed announcement.

But when she arrived at the
palace after school and saw her
parents waiting for her, she knew
they must have some news to
share.

Itty plopped into a chair in the kitchen. Her mom put out some kitty treats and a glass of strawberry milk for an after-school snack, but Itty felt too nervous to enjoy it. Itty explained how she had missed an announcement that morning.

"That's okay," her mother assured her. "The fairy was there to tell you about the royal ball next week. The whole kingdom is invited. And as the new princess, you are hosting!"

"*Everyone?*" Itty asked.

"Everyone!" her father said merrily.

Itty thought for a moment. "Did you say I'm . . . hosting?"

"That simply means you will welcome everyone," the Queen explained.

"Lollyland will want to get to know their princess," the King added.

Itty thought about school today, and how it had been fun to answer her friends' questions.

She didn't love being around big crowds, but maybe this would be okay. Just as long as she didn't have to speak in front of everyone.

Itty let out a deep breath. "Okay." She smiled. "I think I can do that! I was nervous you were going to tell me something—"

"Oh, there's one more thing," the Queen said. "You will perform a dance, and then teach it to everyone. Isn't that exciting?"

Itty let out one tiny nervous squeak. If she hadn't wanted to speak in front of everyone . . . she certainly didn't want to *dance* in front of them!

The Buzz About the Ball

That night Itty had trouble falling asleep. She kept thinking about the dance she was expected to perform in front of a huge crowd.

The thing was, she didn't even know how to dance.

So the thought of performing

a new dance and then having to *teach* it was quite scary.

Itty tossed and turned, nestling deeper in her covers. A soft glowing light caught her eye. Her shooting star! As Itty stared at the warm light, she felt more relaxed.

Maybe no one will even hear about the royal ball, she thought. A wave of sleepiness washed over her. *Maybe no one will come. . . .*

The next morning Itty felt better. She smiled at friends as she walked through the schoolyard.

"Let's all wear matching blue gowns!" she heard Harper say to Fawn and Pansy.

Itty felt a pang in her tummy,

but told herself not to worry. *Maybe they're playing dress-up later.*

"My mom said there hasn't been one since she was my age!" Stella Unicorn, Luna's older sister, cried with glee.

She could be talking about anything, Itty assured herself. *I'll just quietly ask Luna about it when I see her.*

Suddenly glitter was everywhere.

"THE ROYAL BALL IS GOING TO BE AMAZING!" someone yelled.

It was Luna. And she was with Esme and Chipper, who looked as excited as she did.

"Shh!" Itty whispered. "I don't want everyone to hear about the ball."

"Um, everyone already knows," Chipper pointed out.

"Why don't you want anyone to know?" asked Luna. "This is the most exciting news in Lollyland since your shooting star!"

Itty took a deep breath. "As the host of the ball, I have to teach everyone a new dance," she explained.

"That's wonderful," Luna squealed. She didn't yell this time, but she couldn't control the spray of glitter.

"Well, yes, it *would* be wonderful . . . if I knew how to dance," Itty said with a frown.

♥ chapter 5 ♥

A Gown Fit for a Princess

"Dancing is easy-peasy!" Chipper exclaimed.

"Absolutely!" Esme nodded.

But Itty wasn't convinced.

"Don't worry, Itty." Luna grinned at her friend. "We'll give you dance lessons!"

Itty smiled and told her friends the lessons would have to wait. She was set to meet with the royal seamstress that afternoon. The seamstress would be making Itty's dress for the ball.

And no one was more excited about that than Luna, who came home with Itty after school.

"What kind of gown do you want?" Luna asked as they headed up to Itty's room.

Itty wasn't sure. "I think I'll know it when I see it."

As they got to Itty's bedroom, Luna gasped. Speechless, she pointed to a rack in front of Itty's closet. There were dresses upon dresses upon dresses.

"Zat is just one of ze twelve racks I brought!" said someone with an accent that sounded French.

Itty and Luna looked around. Who had said that?

A fashionable-looking poodle emerged from behind the rack. She held out her paw. Itty wasn't sure what to do. Was she supposed to kiss it? Shake it? She decided to curtsy.

"I am Coco, ze royal seamstress," said the dog. "I can also deeee-sign a new gown for you if you

cannot find one here. Are vee ready to begin?"

And so, Itty began. She tried on gown after gown.

There were glittering gowns, silky gowns, rainbow gowns, gowns that changed color, and there was even one with twinkling lights.

"Look at the twinkling lights!"
Luna cheered.

But that one wasn't quite right.
None of them were.

"Perhaps you can tell me vut you like and vut you do not like," Coco suggested.

"Okay . . ." Itty nodded. "I like these colors," she pointed to a rack of pastel gowns. "But I like the fabric on these gowns," she gestured to a rack of fluffy gowns that felt like cotton candy. "Though my gown can't be too poofy, because I need to dance."

Coco was nodding and sketching as Itty spoke.

"Something like thees?" she asked.

Coco had drawn the most perfect gown Itty could imagine.

"Yes, that's it!" Itty purred.

"Now for ze color," Coco said.

"Pink! Or maybe green!" Luna exclaimed.

Itty thought about it. Then she had an idea. She told Coco, who smiled and nodded.

"Good choice, Princess," said the seamstress.

Fancy Footwork

The next day Itty traveled by cloud to Mermaid Cove. She was meeting her friends there for dance lessons.

Mermaid Cove was filled with wonderful sounds—the hum of waterfalls, the singing of mermaids, and the joyful clicking of dolphins in the distance. And then there was the sound of Itty's friends calling her name and clapping as she approached.

"We have three dances to teach you," Chipper said when Itty landed on the ground.

"Me first!" Luna exclaimed. "This is the Unicorn Trot!"

Luna showed her friends a series of quick, twirling steps.

That's some fancy footwork, Itty thought.

"Just follow me," Luna said, and began dancing again, more slowly this time. Itty tried to follow, but her feet wouldn't cooperate. Finally they got so tangled up that she tripped.

"Maybe the Unicorn Trot isn't the right dance for you," Luna said kindly as she helped Itty up.

"Try the Bunny Slide," Chipper called. "It's easy!"

Chipper shimmied around, sliding from side to side and twisting his body. The dance seemed like a lot of fun, and Itty had to admit it did look pretty easy.

But she couldn't quite do it. The steps were simple, but Itty couldn't get that shimmy down.

"I guess it's called the Bunny Slide for a reason," Chipper said. "Maybe it's just meant for bunnies."

"How about the Butterfly Waltz?" Esme fluttered around gracefully. She looked as light as a feather as she danced. As Itty tried to follow along, she realized it was because Esme *was* as light as a feather. Plus, she could fly and Itty couldn't.

Itty's friends didn't know what to do. They were sad they couldn't help her.

"Thanks for trying, guys," Itty said, forcing a smile onto her face.

Her friends smiled back, but they still look concerned.

"Itty, what will you do?" Luna asked. "The ball is in two days!"

Itty tried to act brave. "I'll figure it out."

♥ chapter 7 ♥

Itty Lends
a Paw

Itty couldn't believe the day of
the ball had arrived! She'd spent
yesterday trying to come up with
a simple dance, without much
success.

Dancing just isn't my thing,
Itty thought. She knew it was okay

not to be good at everything, but she wished she was a little better at dancing. She still didn't know what she was going to do when it was time to perform.

Downstairs, the palace was buzzing with activity. Everywhere Itty looked, workers were cleaning, polishing, and setting up for the royal ball.

"Can I help?" Itty asked her mom.

"Oh, Itty, thank you!" the Queen replied. "Could you sweep the hallway? After that, I'm sure the royal decorators could use a paw too."

Itty was happy to help. Having chores to do actually took her mind off dancing. After she swept the hallway, making sure to clean away all the hairballs, she found the royal decorators.

"We can definitely use your climbing skills," one of the palace decorators, a very dapper-looking penguin, said when he saw Itty.

He handed her rolls of gold and silver streamers. "Thanks for your help, Princess!"

Hanging the streamers gave Itty a kitty's-eye view of everything happening below. The floors of the palace gleamed. A bubble machine was being installed, and a rainbow bouncy house was almost inflated.

A team of fairies was setting up
special fountains—a chocolate
fountain, a glitter fountain, and
a frosting fountain. Itty couldn't
decide which fountain she wanted
to try first!

Before long, it was time to get ready for the ball. Everyone in Lollyland would be arriving soon!

Welcome to
the Ball!

Itty heard a scratch at her bedroom door.

A moment later the Queen came in, dressed in a fancy blue velvet gown. Itty did a little twirl to show off her own dress. She hoped her mom would love it as much as she did. It was a beautiful turquoise color. And, in the end, Itty had suggested to the royal seamstress that they add rainbows all over the gown just to make it really special.

"You look wonderful!" her mom purred. "Just one thing is missing!"

Itty frowned.

"Your tiara, of course!" The Queen laughed. She took Itty's tiara from its special box and placed it on her head.

Now Princess Itty was ready for the ball!

"Mom, I'm nervous about my dance," Itty admitted as they headed downstairs. "I'm not the best dancer. What if I disappoint everyone?"

The Queen squeezed Itty's paw. "Just try your best. Our guests are excited to share something special with you. It doesn't have to be perfect."

It doesn't have to be perfect, Itty thought.

Itty and her parents gathered at the palace entrance. The doors swung open and guests began to file in. The line stretched farther than Itty could see. All of Lollyland had come to the ball!

Itty was excited to greet everyone. She chatted happily with a flock of flamingos, and posed for a picture with a group of jaguars.

"Itty, look!"

The King was pointing out a family of dolphins who had just arrived, traveling in special bubbles so they could come on land to join the ball and meet Itty!

Itty's whole school came just in time, too.

"I love your matching gowns!" Itty greeted Fawn, Pansy, and Harper as they arrived together.

Finally Itty spotted her best friends. Luna was wearing a sparkling gown and a glittery tassel on her horn. Chipper wore a checkered tuxedo, and Esme's wings were decorated with shining crystals. With her friends and all the other guests around her in the

palace to celebrate, Itty's heart
swelled with happiness. It was the
perfect start to the royal ball.

Itty just hoped her mom was
right about her *dance* not having
to be perfect . . .
because it was going
to be far from that.

chapter 9

Do the
Itty Dance

"The fountains are so yummy!"
Esme declared.

"The chocolate fountain is my
favorite," Chipper replied. "You
have to try it, Itty!"

"And there's a glitter fountain!"
Luna cried. "So I can get as excited

as I want, and there will be glitter everywhere anyway!"

As Itty giggled, she thought she heard a familiar sound. She twitched her ears to get a better listen.

The Lollyland mermaids were singing. Six notes—that meant it was six o'clock. It was time for the royal family to make their grand entrance and for Itty to perform her dance.

"The fountains will have to wait," Itty said. "I have to go. Wish me luck!"

"You'll do great," her friends cheered.

Itty rushed to the top of the staircase to meet her parents. A hush fell over the crowd as the royal family began their grand entrance.

Then the applause started. The room was filled with meows, barks, whinnies, quacks, chirps, and oinks . . . all the sounds of Lollyland as everyone cheered.

At the bottom of the stairs Itty's parents stepped aside. It was time for Itty to dance.

Just try your best. It doesn't have to be perfect.

The music started and Itty took
a deep breath. She had a plan,
sort of. She was going to start
with a twirl, then do a few steps
of the Unicorn Trot, and then a
little slide from the Bunny Slide.

Itty twirled to the beat.

She took one step, and a second step . . . and then moved to the left. But not on purpose! She'd slipped on some frosting that had spilled over from the fountain.

Itty wiggled her arms as she slid across the floor, trying to keep her balance.

She leaped to avoid crashing into the band, somehow managed to twirl around, and landed in a deep bow, sort of like a curtsy.

Itty stood up and waited in her spot.

The music had stopped.

The room was silent.

Then something wonderful happened. Everyone burst into applause. Loud, wild applause! Everyone in Lollyland loved Itty's dance! The band began playing

again, and animals rushed onto the dance floor, twirling, sliding, and wiggling their arms.

"Do the Princess Itty!" the bandleader cried.

A Sweet Ending

Halfway through the ball, the dance floor was still packed. Lollyland was twirling, sliding, leaping, and curtsying. Itty decided it was a good time to take a break and look for her friends.

As she walked around the royal

ballroom, Lollylanders who weren't
dancing rushed over to meet her.

"Can we take a picture with
you?" some asked.

"We loved seeing your shooting
star, Princess Itty!" others said.

But one thing almost everyone
wanted to tell Itty was how much
they loved her dance.

Itty spotted a spray of glitter across the room, nowhere near the glitter fountain. Sure enough, Luna was there. She, Esme, and Chipper were chatting excitedly.

"Itty! You did it!" Esme and Chipper cheered as they saw her approaching.

Luna rushed forward to hug her best friend. "That was the best dance *ever*!" Luna exclaimed. "How did you come up with it?"

"Can you guys keep a secret?"
Itty giggled. "My dance was a
mistake. I slipped in the frosting
and everything that happened
was totally an accident!"

"Best mistake *ever!*" Luna shouted. The four friends laughed as glitter rained down on them.

"Look over there!" Esme cried, pointing across the ballroom. A dragon was blowing beautiful flames into whatever shape the guests asked him to.

In another corner, a monkey balloon artist was creating the coolest balloon animals Itty had ever seen. She watched as the monkey shaped and twisted a balloon. A small kitten was waiting patiently for him to finish. Soon the balloon took on a familiar shape. It was a balloon version of Princess Itty, dressed in her gown and tiara!

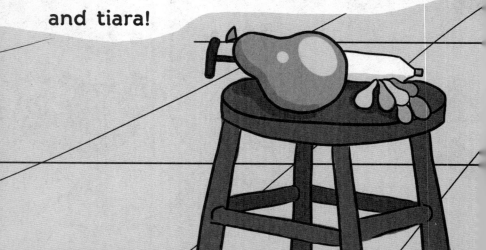

Just then, Itty's tummy rumbled
so loud her friends turned to look
at her.

"Are you thinking what I'm thinking?" Itty asked her friends.

"To the chocolate fountain!" they cried.

1. Twirl!

2. Step!   3. Step!

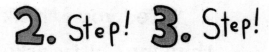

5. Jump!

6. Twirl!

4. Slide!

7. Land!

8. Curtsy!

Here's a sneak peek at Itty's next royal adventure!

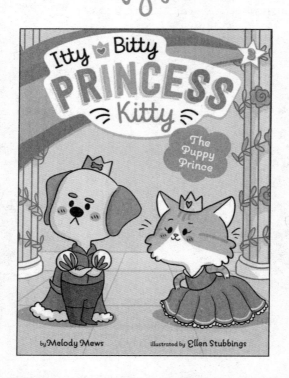

Itty ♥ Bitty
PRINCESS
Kitty

The Puppy Prince

by Melody Mews   illustrated by Ellen Stubbings

Itty Bitty Princess Kitty was concentrating very hard. Her legs twitched as she focused on the platform across from her. It was so far away! But she'd seen her parents, the Queen and King of Lollyland, make this jump many times.

You can do this, Itty told herself.

Just then, a flash of movement

outside the window caught her eye. She blinked. Was that . . . a *dragon*?

Itty leaped down and raced out of the climbing room. She skidded to a stop in the grand hall, where her parents were standing in front of the palace doors.

"Mom! Dad!" Itty took a deep breath. "There's a DRAGON outside! Run!"

Queen Kitty smiled. "Yes, darling," she purred. "No need to worry—or run. It's an announcement dragon from Wagmire!"